December DESIRE

HALLIE BENNETT

BOOKS BY THIS AUTHOR

Standalones
Batter Up
Wood Lessons
Tees & Jeans Series
The Brother Bias
The Boss Bias
The Bad Boy Bias
Lumberjacks of High Ridge Series
Kept by the Beast
Claimed by the Woodsman
Found by the Loner
Curvy College Reunion Series
Campus Good Girl
Campus Queen
Campus Bookworm
Campus Professor
Christmas & Curves Series
Festive Fever
December Desire
Mountain Men of Suitor's Crossing Series
A Date with the Mountain Man

For those "Hallmark After Dark" fans who are crushing on a network's Golden Boy. ☺

CHAPTER ONE

MADDIE

"I can't believe we're actually here." After a two-hour flight from Nashville, it's surreal to finally attend MerryCon—a gathering of holiday film super fans intent on meeting their favorite small-screen celebrities.

And at the top of my list? Calder Mayfield—everyone's Hallmark crush and all-around good guy judging by the interviews I've seen him give.

"Same." Lola agrees, her pink pixie cut practically glowing with nervous energy. "We're lucky you snagged the few remaining tickets for the weekend. Can you imagine being stuck at home and seeing everyone else share their pictures? I would've died of envy." A dramatic hand covers her heart as we navigate to the end of Calder's line once a volunteer admits us into the main arena.

Laughing at my best friend's theatrics, I crane my neck over a tinsel barrier to gauge how long it'll be before we reach his booth for photos. The information online recommended fans arrive an hour earlier than MerryCon officially started to ensure an opportunity to meet the famous actor, and after reading disgruntled comments about some fans missing their chance due to time running out, Lola and I made sure to get here as soon as possible.

"How long do you think we'll have to wait?" I ask a little while later, switching my weight to my other leg. Already my feet are hurting in the cute boots I decided to wear.

"Probably hours with how slow this is moving. Why? Eager to meet Prince Charming?" Lola teases me with her nickname for Calder since he's played an inordinate number of royal characters in his movies—not to mention the way I've idealized him as my dream man.

"Obviously... But at the moment I'm more concerned with my feet's pain level. I never should've worn these boots; it was stupid to think dressing up would catch his attention, especially in the sea of women here." Familiar insecurity wraps around my heart and squeezes. It's no secret how shy I am around men, preferring to fade into the background to protect myself from their judgment. As a thirty-year-old virgin whose double-digit jeans size starts with a two, my mind can't help creating humiliating scenes of rejection from any man I'm interested in.

Calder Mayfield included.

Although it helps knowing nothing could form between us since he's a celebrity and I'm not. He'll be polite when I meet him, we'll take a smiling photo, and I can continue thinking of him as the perfect guy for me until a real one materializes. The only thing I truly fear when it's my turn to greet him is stammering over my words and looking like a tomato from blushing so fiercely.

"Beauty is pain..." Lola says sagely before patting my arm in encouragement. "Don't worry, you'll be fine. Keep imagining the moment when Calder sees you and falls in love. Then it'll all be worth it. Besides, you know I wouldn't let you leave the hotel

looking anything but hot, so stop sweating these other women. They've got nothing on you, girl."

"Thanks," I murmur, shooting a grateful glance her way, though I'm still not convinced. We're both romantics at heart which is why we love these holiday romances from Hallmark, Lifetime, and the Hearts of America Channel or HAC. However, Lola tends to be more optimistic, choosing to believe that the magic of Christmas is on our side. "But enough about me. What about you and Macy Adams? Don't tell me you're not feeling nervous about meeting the woman of *your* dreams."

"No comment." Lola crosses her arms defiantly, chin jutting out in challenge, daring me to push the topic. "This is Calder's line and your moment to shine—not mine."

Hmm... maybe not as optimistic as I thought.

"Fine, but your time's coming..." I warn. We had two motives for coming to MerryCon this year: meeting our individual crushes, Calder Mayfield and Macy Adams, and exploring New York City which is an hour's train ride from here. Calder will be checked off the list soon, then it'll be Macy's turn.

As we near the front of the queue, I shrug out of my coat and drape it over my arm, pulling at the sweater dress underneath to relieve some of the heat that's gathered.

Calm down. Now's not the time to become a sweaty mess.

The black tights meant as another layer of protection from the weather chafes along my thighs, and my discomfort grows.

Calder's voice drifts above the crowd, the deep baritone overcoming the chatter and calling every single one of my nerves to attention. Glimpses of his smiling face peek through the windows of space opened by shifting fans. Classically handsome with golden blonde hair and ice-blue eyes, he exudes an

All-American persona that fits perfectly with the characters he plays on Hallmark and Lifetime.

"What's your name?" A woman in a volunteer shirt steps forward and writes our names on a yellow sticky note after we answer, handing it to me and moving on to the next group. Guess this pushes guests through the meet and greet more efficiently if we don't have to bother with niceties like saying who we are.

When it's our turn to meet Calder, a wave of nausea kicks me in the gut. I'm overheating—probably flushed from head to toe—while my outfit's rubbing me in all the wrong places, amping my anxiety up to the max.

What is wrong with me?

He's just a man. A famous one, but still human. Yet I'm acting like he's a mythical creature who won't forget my name the moment I leave.

"I'll take your phones, and you can put the rest of your things on that chair before standing by Mr. Mayfield for your photo." Another volunteer gestures to a spare chair where Lola and I drop our coats and purses.

This is it. The moment I've been waiting for.

"Hi, Maddie, Lola. It's nice to meet you!" Calder shakes each of our hands, and an electrical shock shoots up my arm. We both jerk back with awkward laughs, his light eyes crinkling at the corners, while Lola spies from the side, a triumphant look on her face.

Embarrassed, I abruptly apologize before launching into what I'd practiced saying to him. "Thank you for doing this! Your movies are our favorite, especially *Love in Hollybrook*."

"Yeah, Maddie loves that one. We've watched it too many times to count," Lola interjects, rolling her eyes exasperatedly.

Like we don't watch Macy's Mistletoe Madness *just as often...*

Calder's interest centers on me—the force of his full attention rendering me speechless. "*Love in Hollybrook*? That was one of my first holiday projects for HAC. I didn't realize they still played it since it's been so long. I'm impressed you've seen it."

Another blush rises to the surface at his praise, and I surreptitiously brush the back of my hand across my forehead, pretending to swipe at a stray hair. Alarm rushes through me at the slight dampness of sweat. *Nauseous, feverish...* Have I worked myself into the beginnings of an anxiety attack?

Struggling to slow the chaos erupting in my body, I take a deep, measured breath and force myself to remember that I'm safe—not in danger. Calder's a man I'll never see again, so worrying about what to say or how I look isn't helpful.

Just act normal, take the picture, then you're done. Safe and sound.

"It's a *clate*—I mean *great*... Sorry, I thought 'classic' then 'great' and combined them." A nervous giggle bubbles over before I manage to stammer out a few more words, scrubbing clammy hands over the skirt of my dress. "It's a cute film. More people should see it."

Lola's expression switches from encouraging to concerned as she witnesses my crumbling composure. Shooting a pleading glance her way, she steps forward to divert the conversation, but the volunteer motions for us to gather in a line with Calder in the middle. "Sorry to interrupt, but your time is up. We need to snap the photo and usher the next guests in."

Nodding, I stand to Calder's right while he wraps an arm around my back, the warm weight hovering over me, so his heat is the only thing touching my body. *Like a true gentleman.* Crisp pine tickles my nose, and I can't resist tilting my head closer to breathe it in more deeply—the fresh fragrance comforting, offering clarity to my muddled, anxious mind.

"There you go! You're all set!" Our phones are returned to us as we retrieve our things, and someone steers us away. With a faint wave of farewell, Lola and I leave Calder behind as he greets another round of fans, though I swear I feel his lingering stare as we exit.

It's just your imagination.

"Well, that was fun..."

"If you consider standing on the brink of an anxiety attack *fun*," I mutter. "I shouldn't have worked myself into a fit when I knew our meeting wouldn't be a big deal. It was hardly five minutes!"

Weaving through other celebrities' lines and various Christmas trees set up around the area, I snag an empty seat at a table in the concessions court, plopping into the metal chair with relief.

"How are you feeling now?" Lola's brows knit together over her hazel eyes, worry stamped in the grim line of her mouth.

Holiday music plays overhead while a brisk outdoor breeze flows in from a vendor carrying a load of ornaments. Both aid the calming of my nerves as my body begins to settle into a normal rhythm. "Better. Let's just sit here for a while longer until it fades a bit more."

"Whatever you need. I'll just post our pic with Calder so everyone can be jealous."

Shaking my head at her silliness, I continue counting my breaths. *Inhale. One. Exhale. Two.* At least I've come a long way since starting therapy. Already my body's reactions are slowing, returning to base level, when before an attack might affect me for an entire day, if not longer.

Taking pride in my progress, I relax in my seat and congratulate myself on surviving the introduction to Calder, too.

Now that we've met, my crush is stronger than ever—even if I did briefly botch our conversation. He was every bit as handsome and friendly as I imagined, and with the anxiety symptoms finally fading, I'm free to bask in the memory of actually meeting Calder Mayfield—the Prince Charming of my dreams.

CHAPTER TWO

CALDER

During a mandated break from meeting fans, I finally have time to silence all my phone's notifications. It's been pinging nonstop, and the annoying vibration is threatening to ruin my good mood.

Granted, most of the notifications are tags from fans as they share their photos with me—something I'm intensely grateful for—but it's beginning to distract me from genuinely interacting with them in person.

"I don't know how you live like that." The volunteer assigned to me, Megan, gestures to the continuous noise coming from my cell, bewilderment written on her face.

"It can be overwhelming at times, but you learn how to live with it. Besides, as long as this is going off like a damn tuning fork it means people still care about me which is essential in this line of business."

Networks love me and keep sending projects my way—mostly due to the popularity of my films with their core audiences. Christened as one of Hallmark's "It" Men, plum roles land in my lap before most of the other leads even hear of them.

"But shouldn't you have an assistant who takes care of those sorts of things?"

"I do, but I like to keep tabs on my personal accounts, to stay connected to my fans instead of relying on someone else to double as me." It's the least I can do when people take the time to post their appreciation of me and my movies.

I scroll the mass of DMs and tags until one catches my eye—Maddie, the pretty but flustered woman from earlier. She'd surprised me with her knowledge of *Love in Hollybrook*, not to mention the effect her sweater-wrapped curves had on my body, despite it encountering beautiful women all the time. Hell, I met over a dozen just today, yet something about Maddie stuck with me.

The picture leads to her friend's profile where she tagged Maddie as well. Following the trail like a hound on the hunt, I find the correct account, though it's set to private. The small circle by her handle reveals a smiling Maddie, a sweet but tempting sight, and I debate my next move.

Message her.

And then what?

Starting anything with a fan is a recipe for disaster—and possibly dangerous. *It's not like she's a stalker.* Nixing that ridiculous possibility, my mind turns to the more reasonable scenario: I'm likely to be taken advantage of... again.

As much as I love and respect women, yearning to spoil those in my care, it's no secret that I have a terrible track record when it comes to relationships.

Girlfriends who try to take advantage of every perk my celebrity affords them.

Women who are more concerned with material products than me.

The list goes on.

Except now I want to add a fan who messes up her words and blushes in my company, who'd probably prefer the image of me from television rather than the actual man.

Send the damn message. Where's the harm in seeing what happens?

For all I know, the conversation will fizzle out after some back and forth, allowing me to focus on the rest of MerryCon—free of wondering about Maddie. *Then, it's decided.* A quick line of greeting is sent before I overthink it again.

Not five minutes later, an answer buzzes on my phone, and my pulse picks up speed when her name crosses the screen.

MADDIE: Hi! And same! Thanks for attending MerryCon and making that movie. It's such a beautiful story! Hope you're able to relax some this weekend; I'm sure it can be overwhelming having to meet so many people at once.

A smiling emoji ends the text, and I can't help a burgeoning warmth due to the compassionate note at the end. It's sweet of her to worry about how I'm feeling, to try to empathize with my situation.

CALDER: Thankfully, the organizers built in break times for us, so we're not going nonstop all weekend.

Considering the upcoming lunch break at noon, a wild idea takes root, and I quickly type out the spontaneous suggestion.

CALDER: My lunch is scheduled for noon... Would you like to join me?

Three dots appear.

Then the screen goes blank.

Come on, Maddie. Say yes.

The cycle repeats again until one line comes through: ***Sure! Do I need a special pass or anything?***

Success! I'm still confused about why it's so important to see Maddie again, but there's no denying the sense of victory stampeding through my veins. Maybe it's been too long since I've had a woman. Or maybe all this Christmas spirit surrounding me has my head thinking we're really living in a holiday movie. Either way, I'm not one to retreat from something I want—no matter how little sense it might make.

CALDER: *I'll take care of everything. Just stop by the double doors under the giant "Welcome to the North Pole" banner at noon. Can't wait to talk again!*

WHEN LUNCHTIME ROLLS around, the line of people waiting for photos with me still extends past the official entrance to the queue, and it's clear I'll be late meeting Maddie. I shoot off a quick text of apology before relaying a new plan, asking one of my volunteers to escort her into the area reserved for celebrities and their entourages while I finish up here.

"Last one," I murmur to Megan who nods as she takes the next guest's camera.

Fifteen minutes go by with no end in sight as the line continues to grow. We need to pause now, otherwise, there's no doubt we'll work straight through lunch—something I'm not willing to do with Maddie waiting for me.

After a final wave of goodbye, I hustle towards the celebrity holding area, dodging exuberant fans and inflated snowmen standing as sentry by certain booths. A security guard posted outside closed double-doors checks my MerryCon pass before allowing me entry into a room buzzing with animated chatter.

My gaze lands on Maddie who's alone at a round table until Marsha Kent and her husband near two empty seats. Heading their way, I overhear the beginning of their conversation.

"Hi! I don't think we've met. I'm Marsha, and this is Dillon. Do you mind if we sit with you?"

"Sure, it's no problem. I'm just waiting for someone."

Releasing a breath, she passes a subtle test: choosing not to mention me, allowing me to remain anonymous instead of using my name for clout. Not that Marsha Kent isn't a household name in her own right, but it's still a mark in Maddie's favor.

"Hey, sorry I'm late. It was difficult finding a lull between guests. Should we grab something to eat before it's all gone?" I motion towards long tables stacked with sandwiches, chips, and other assorted sides before asking Marsha, "Do you mind saving our seats while we're gone?"

She waves us away with an encouraging smile, her gaze bouncing between Maddie and me. I can tell she's storing up a load of questions to ask when we're alone since I rarely bring dates to events like these.

Marsha is a mother hen and has been in the entertainment business for as long as I've been alive. A living legend, she takes her roles seriously—on and off the screen, which includes offering advice or a shoulder to lean on to her younger co-stars.

"So, you've seen *Love in Hollybrook*, but what's your favorite part?" I ask, hoping to ease into conversation by mentioning something I already know she likes.

Maddie considers her answer, grabbing a turkey sandwich and a bag of Lays from the available refreshments. "This is going to sound like I'm brownnosing, but I swear it's the truth. My favorite thing about the movie was your character's persistence in voicing his feelings. He was upfront about how he felt instead of denying it."

"I liked that about him, too. Life's too short to hold back and hide when you're in love with someone. Or even attracted to them."

Which is why I messaged you.

"In theory, I agree with you." She shrugs before snagging a bottle of water. "But in practice, it's a bit harder to achieve."

We slowly walk back to the table with our hands full, and I grin, gently bumping her elbow with mine. "I don't know. You seem to be doing a pretty good job of it right now... at least I hope so. Because that's why I asked you to join me for lunch. You're beautiful, and I couldn't stop thinking about you."

I hear the catch in her breath and fear maybe I came on too strong. But I'm a straightforward kind of guy. And we're living on borrowed time anyway with MerryCon ending tomorrow.

I want her to know where I stand.

Maddie's toe catches on an invisible crack on the floor as she stumbles in surprise, sending her lunch flying to the ground. Immediately, I drop my own food and reach out to stop her forward momentum. Our arms entangle—Maddie trying to catch herself while I'm trying to catch her—and we end up falling into an inflatable reindeer to our left, the poor creature deflating in slow motion as we're swallowed within its plastic depths.

"Mr. Mayfield, are you okay?" Multiple concerned voices erupt at once, but my concentration is centered on the curvy little bundle who lies still at my side.

"Maddie, sweetheart, are you hurt?"

"No, just catching my breath..." Finally, she rolls to face me, disheveled hair sticking to her face and the downed reindeer in a spiky halo. Scarlet flushes her skin and not only because of the big red Rudolph nose hovering near her cheek. "I'm *sapolog*... I mean I'm sorry. I didn't mean to ruin your break."

It's adorable how she mixes her words together, although I hate that it seems to appear when she's nervous or embarrassed. "You haven't ruined anything. These damn holiday decorations are everywhere. Someone was bound to have an accident eventually. I'm just glad you're alright."

The thin plastic of the deflated reindeer starts separating from us as people attempt an extraction, and instinctively, my hand goes to Maddie's cheek, swiping at the tendrils of amber refusing to settle, too full of static electricity.

"I must look like a mess." Her hand joins mine, our skin touching and rekindling the spark from earlier when we first met.

"You look gorgeous considering a reindeer attempted to take you out." And still trying, apparently, because a few parts around us keep trying to re-inflate. Why hasn't someone shut this thing down yet?

A wry chuckle erases some of the mortification from her expression, and it pleases me to lessen her embarrassment, even in a small way.

"Is this what happens when Rudolph is your least favorite reindeer?"

"Ah, Revenge of Rudolph the Red-Nosed Reindeer... Guess they don't play that one on Hallmark, hmm?" I quip.

"For good reason, apparently. He's a vindictive little creature." She lifts a few strands of hair and makes a silly face. "The bearer of bad hair days."

Laughing at her playful banter, I return to smoothing the mussed wisps when flashes of light pop in the background. Cameras are taking shot after shot of us, and Maddie realizes it at the same time, her teasing smile disappearing as she ducks her head.

"Come on, let's get out of here." I wrap an arm around her shoulders and guide her away from the scene of our accident, but an escape fails to materialize.

We're in a large conference room in a warehouse. There's only the exit outside—home to wintry weather that we're not prepared for—or the double doors back to the main MerryCon floor.

"Mr. Mayfield, who's your friend?"

"Calder, give us a smile with your girlfriend!"

Paparazzi isn't supposed to be back here, but clearly, they managed to weasel their way inside. And now they're intent on hounding us until they get an answer. Rudolph might become my least favorite reindeer, too, after drawing attention to me and Maddie.

Knowing what I need to do, I hurry towards the double doors. "Sweetheart, I hate to cut our date short, but I need to deal with these reporters. I'll block the doors and stop them from following you, so you can safely escape. But I'll DM you, okay?"

Damn, I didn't even have time to get her number.

"Alright... Are you sure you'll be fine?"

"Yeah, baby. I've got this. I'll talk to you later." With a final wave, I get her safely through the doors before facing the group of men hounding us. Forcing a friendly smile, I prepare to be nice instead of telling them to *fuck off*. This is a family event, after all.

"Five minutes, guys. Then I've gotta eat before getting back to my fans."

And messaging Maddie.

The short time we spent together wasn't enough.

I need more.

CHAPTER THREE

Maddie

I find Lola sampling fudge at a vendor's booth after taking a restroom detour to fix myself due to the reindeer snafu. Her mouth's full of chocolate, but that doesn't stop her from pouncing the moment I'm within earshot.

"How was it? What's he like?"

Shrugging nonchalantly—as if internally I'm not completely giddy and anxious all at the same time—I accept one of the white fudge samples offered to me. "We didn't get to talk much because I crushed an inflatable reindeer."

"You... What?" She chokes and coughs, a hand covering her mouth.

"Calder and I were walking back to our table when he called me *beautiful*, then I kind of blanked out and tripped into him and a blow-up Rudolph decoration. He was really sweet about the accident, but then a group of paparazzi caught us off-guard. Calder ushered me out as fast as possible."

The flash of blinding lights mimicked a scene straight from a movie—nosy photographers looking for a scoop, a hero guiding the damsel to safety.

Geez, he's not really a prince, you know.

Lola stares at me in shock, standing speechless for once. "Wow."

"Yeah."

"What happens now?"

Recounting Calder's promise to message me, I add, "Plus, he called our lunch a *date*. That means something right?" It felt like it did. Like I'm more than just another fan in his eyes. Like he actually sees me as an attractive woman—one he wants to get to know for longer than a weekend.

Don't get too far ahead of yourself.

It's difficult to imagine a man like him desiring me when so many others have either overlooked me or outright rejected me because of my weight.

And while I normally wouldn't accept a man's compliments so easily, there's something about the brevity of this weekend and Calder's personality that has my fearful, doubtful side fading to the background.

"Hell yes, it does." Lola squeals before throwing her arms around me in an exuberant hug. "I'm jealous and so happy for you!"

Laughing at the mock envy on her face, I steal another fudge sample from the Santa plate sitting on the vendor's table before buying an assorted box of flavors for later. A little celebration gift to myself for being brave and optimistic about Calder.

You'd think the reindeer debacle would've completely derailed my weekend—and granted, at the time I wanted to disappear out of embarrassment—but the good things that came of it somehow outweigh the mortification.

Calder swept me away from danger, or at least a hoard of prying paparazzi, and he carefully checked on my well-being, concern emanating from him rather than judgment or annoyance at my fall. Maybe it's just the spirit of the season, but I'm finding it difficult to ignore the good things.

Maybe it's your anxiety meds and therapy doing their job.

Either way, I'll take it.

After perusing the rest of the vendor booths, Lola and I meander through the crowd of people, contemplating our next stop. MerryCon is full of celebrities to meet and vendors to visit, but it also hosts workshops and panels—everything holiday-themed and meant to keep attendees entertained for an entire weekend, though we're only here for today.

We would've liked to attend more days, but tickets were hard to come by. Apparently, come December, this is the hottest place to be for holiday rom-com fans, which is why Lola and I planned a mini-vacation to New York City tomorrow in lieu of MerryCon.

Suddenly, my phone vibrates with a notification. "It's from Calder," I say, reading the short paragraph he sent. "He wants to know if I'll go with him to see *The Nutcracker* tomorrow."

"Oh, the ballet. Fancy!" Lola hums in approval and points toward a sign highlighting a contest about to happen. Calder's name is in bold block letters next to a couple of other listed celebrities. "Let's grab some hot cocoa to go with this fudge, then head over for the gingerbread house contest since it's about to start. We can watch your man compete and discuss clothing options."

"He's not my man."

"*Yet*. But a romantic night in the city will change that real quick."

A girl can dream.

Buying our drinks plus a hot dog since my lunch went haywire, we sit in the last row of chairs for the contest, content with having empty seats as a buffer around us while we chat and watch.

The first gingerbread house is Macy's, and I nudge Lola. "Hey look, there's *your* girl." Macy walks out in a red dress to match an adorable cottage with red gumdrops on its roof. The creative confection is wheeled to the judges' table before another celebrity and their house follows.

"Her house is really cute."

"Yeah, and so is she," I push, determined to encourage her crush after my experience with Calder. If an awkward girl like me can land *his* attention, then there's hope for Lola with her bright personality.

"And what about Calder?" The man in question follows a cart toting his house—a two-story concoction of peppermint sticks and licorice. "You need to ask him if he really made that because it looks too good."

"Probably all the movie practice." Though she's got a point. It resembles a professionally finished home some baker would make on the Food Network.

Proof he's good with his hands.

A heated blush accompanies the thought, but it's hard to resist imagining what those skilled fingers would feel like on my skin. Would they be rough? Smooth? Definitely warm.

As if my body wouldn't already be on fire for him.

"Sadly, that hasn't helped Eli Cooper. I'm worried his roof's about to cave in." Lola's comment interrupts me from spiraling into a sexual fantasy in the middle of MerryCon, and I'm grateful for the distraction. I don't need to be walking around with wet panties for the next few hours.

"Let's hope it doesn't." Eli joined the ranks of holiday rom-com stars a few years ago, and while I've liked his movies, there's always been an attitude about him that makes me wary.

Like he thinks he's too good for Hallmark or Lifetime movies and only does them for the money.

Which I understand, but also... Where's your appreciation for the season? The fans? It just feels judgmental to me, although it's not like I personally know the guy.

Maybe you can ask Calder what he's really like later.

We watch for a few more minutes before it becomes obvious that Macy will win, so we switch over to discussing our plans for tomorrow.

"This is perfect. We'll be in New York City, one of the fashion capitals of the world, and we can find you a gown that Calder won't be able to resist ripping off you."

"Hopefully this dress is cheap if it's meant to end in tatters," I quip, crumpling the wrapper of my eaten hot dog and tossing it in my purse.

"Tell me you did not just say that. Tell me you're not thinking about money instead of being naked in front of your dream man—your freaking Prince Charming."

Rolling my eyes at her theatrics, I smirk. "I can think of both. Though my biggest concern is finding something to fit. You know that's the most difficult part." The amusement fades from my tone as I consider past shopping expeditions that ended in failure. Homecoming. Prom. Bridesmaid gowns where I had to buy a slightly altered version of what everyone else wore due to my size.

Lola pats my arm in sympathy. "I know, but I also refuse to believe your Cinderella weekend can be thwarted by a dress. Christmas magic is in the air. We'll find something."

Crossing my fingers, I pray she's right then snicker. "If I'm Cinderella, does that mean you're my fairy godmother?"

"Fairy godsister, thank you. I'm too young to be a mother."

"You're not but okay..." I grin, knowing her commitment to remaining child-free.

Calder's voice draws my attention as he answers a fan's question, and I admire his lean physique—on display in casual jeans and blazer, even at this distance. And I'm sucked back into daydreaming. About earlier. About tomorrow.

He's so handsome and sweet. The protective way he'd wrapped his arms around me during my fall... It almost makes me believe in Lola's claim of Christmas magic. Because I certainly feel smitten. In a real way now that I've met Calder.

He's no longer a pipe dream or fictional character.

Which means he has the very real power to break my heart.

CHAPTER FOUR

CALDER

Snow starts to fall as I wait for Maddie outside her hotel like she requested, insisting it wasn't necessary for me to escort her down from her hotel room. The gentleman in me protested, but she wouldn't relent. So here I stand, roses in hand with white snowflakes dusting my shoulders—a bundle of nerves—like a middle school boy escorting a girl to his first dance.

For the past twenty-four hours, Maddie's all that's been on my mind. Through every meet and greet with fans. Through the panel I was a part of today. She was never far from my thoughts, and I made damn sure I stayed in hers, too, by messaging her whenever I found a moment of respite.

I offered passes for MerryCon today, hoping to see her before tonight's date, but she'd explained how she and her friend already had plans to explore New York City. Understanding though disappointed, my day dragged on without her presence.

But you'll have tonight with her.

First, *The Nutcracker* in Lincoln Center then dinner afterward at Cafe Fiorello.

I want tonight to be special for Maddie, especially since we have a limited amount of time together, which means going all out with the romance and showing how I feel. Although I'm hoping our connection won't end this weekend.

The hotel doors slide open, and Maddie appears—a beautiful vision in shimmering green, an emerald princess. Sheer sleeves cover her arms while a deep vee and high slit in the skirt showcase her curves, and I'm dumbstruck with need.

To hold her.

To love her.

To make her mine.

My lungs drag in a harsh breath of cold air, burning an icy hot path in my chest. If it were up to me, we'd skip the ballet and head straight to my suite at the Plaza Hotel. I don't want anyone else around us. I don't want an audience.

Maddie's all I desire.

"Hi..." She shyly waves while carefully toeing through the thin layer of snow on the ground. Shaken from my stupor, I return her greeting and rush over to guide her safely to my car rental.

"You are stunning. A winter princess." Corny but true. Maddie looks like she could've stepped off the set of a royal holiday movie, the leading lady to my character. "These are for you." She brings the roses to her nose and smiles.

"Thank you." A becoming flush of scarlet completes her holiday ensemble, and I can't resist dropping a kiss on the back of her hand after settling her into the passenger seat. "I suppose that's fitting considering how many princes you've played."

I chuckle, rounding the car before getting in the driver's seat. Maddie seems lighter than when I first met her, not quite as nervous, and I hope it's because our conversations over the phone have eased some of her misgivings about dating a celebrity. Let alone her celebrity crush—a fact she'd reluctantly shared when I'd asked who she'd been most excited to meet at MerryCon.

The hour-long drive into the city flies by as we discuss theater productions we've been to. Maddie's seen *Wicked* but would love to attend a showing of *The Lion King*, while my favorite musical is *Hamilton*. It's funny learning where our interests overlap and where they differ—playful debates springing forth in defense of our unique tastes.

There's a decent crowd filing into the David H. Koch Theater when we arrive, and we find our seats on the second tier when Maddie pauses, her mouth thinning into a disappointed line.

"What's wrong?"

She looks at me then downward, twisting the matching handbag in her hands. "The seats are small."

I glance between her and the seats and realize what she means. Armrests line each side, and it's obvious they form more of a cage around a person rather than providing comfort. It's never occurred to me to question a seat's size. Or to wonder if it's accessible for everyone.

But now my privilege is glaring in my face. As is guilt.

"I'm sorry. I didn't think..."

"No, you don't need to apologize." Maddie's eyes sparkle under the dim lights, tears of shame threatening to fall, a sight that breaks my heart and causes a well of protectiveness to charge forward.

"I'll fix this. Wait here." Leaving, I approach an attendant and ask for different accommodations. Surely, we're not the first couple to arrive and discover their woefully lacking seat size.

"This is all we have, sir." The young man carries a larger metal chair with no armrests but no other sign of comfort either, except for the mediocre cushion gracing its seat.

I want to snap at him. How could a world-class facility such as this not have anything better for its patrons? But his defeated expression stops a forthcoming tirade.

It's not his fault; he's only one employee trying to do his job.

Sighing, I nod and guide him back to our seats where he wedges the substitute accommodation in front of the two chairs. It's a tight fit, and I hear whispers from the guests behind us.

If only we had a private box.

"This was all they had," I explain. "Which is unacceptable, and I'll completely understand if you want to leave."

Maddie bites her lip in indecision before a self-deprecating laugh bubbles up. "I've always wanted to see *The Nutcracker* in New York City... Just my luck that I'm too big to sit down."

"You're perfect the way you are. You're not the problem. The theater wants to house as many people as possible for shows because that's how they make money, which means they make the seats smaller to fit more in. That's on them, not you."

"I appreciate the rationalization even if I don't quite believe I'm not responsible for causing an issue." Maddie sighs and a tight smile tugs at her lips. "This chair's fine, though I'm not sure how comfortable you'll be with it taking up so much of your leg room."

"Well, I've got a solution for that." I maneuver around the limited space and sit in the metal chair before gently pulling Maddie onto my lap. Instinctively, her arms wrap around my neck for balance, her fingers clenching in my hair.

"What are you doing?" she hisses as more disgruntled comments emerge from behind. I'm about to tell the disrespectful jerks to shut up or get out.

"Making sure we're both comfortable." My hands smooth over her legs, finding the slit of her dress and diving beneath to caress her bare thigh.

Maddie jumps at the touch, pressing her chest closer to mine—the soft bounty of her breasts a delicious distraction. "This can't possibly be comfortable for you. This show is two hours long. Your legs will be numb by the end."

"A sacrifice I'm willing to make because I'm not letting you move from this spot. You're too much of a tempting handful."

And however much I hate the circumstances leading to this point, it's certainly pushed us into close quarters sooner than I expected—a fact I wholly appreciate.

The orchestra begins playing the opening notes of Tchaikovsky, silencing a rebuttal from Maddie, but I feel her anxiety in the stiffness of her muscles, spine rigid beneath my palm.

This won't do.

As the velvet curtains part to reveal a cozy room decorated for Christmas, I focus on relaxing Maddie, so she can actually enjoy the ballet. Massaging along each vertebra. Featherlight caresses along her inner thigh. Nuzzling whisper-soft kisses in the crook of her neck.

Like the first thaw of spring, she slowly melts in my arms, her lush body leaning more heavily into mine as her breathing becomes deeper, her temperature rising. I swear I can almost smell her arousal through the cloud of perfume and cologne floating in the air from the other guests.

The Nutcracker and Mouse King are fighting on stage, but it's my heart beating overtime to the swelling melody of their battle. I wish I could whisk Maddie away to a private alcove. Wish I could taste her slick arousal on my tongue.

But I won't ruin this for her.

This is a bucket list item for her; she said so in an earlier message.

So, I'll bide my time with delicate touches until I'm free to release my hunger.

To claim my curvy little princess.

CHAPTER FIVE

MADDIE

The ballet was beautiful.

Dinner was delicious.

But now that Calder and I are snuggled beneath a blanket in a horse carriage driving us through Central Park, the fairytale is nearing its end, and I don't want it to. My body is primed for more, thanks to Calder's relentless campaign of innocent grazes and not-so-innocent caresses during the ballet.

I barely had time to lament the awkward situation about the theater chair being too small for my hips and ass before he solved the issue and pulled me onto his lap—his firm thighs and chest cushioning me against his warmth.

The casual way he did it, like we've been in a relationship for years rather than on our first date, caught me off guard. A man's never held me before. I've never sat in a guy's lap even for a moment, too self-conscious about my weight.

But Calder didn't care.

And to prove it, his wandering hands kindled a flame of lust in my belly, overriding the pit of embarrassment. A fire that slowly spread outward as he continued to touch me with knowing skill. Touches that didn't stop after the ballet ended. No, even at Cafe Fiorello, a popular restaurant for ballet goers, Calder sat next to me, his heated gaze devouring me as if I were on the menu instead of spicy Italian food.

"What are you thinking?" Calder asks, his breath frosting in the air.

"Nothing really. Just replaying the night. I think this may be the perfect date, though I guess I shouldn't expect anything less from rom-com's golden boy Calder Mayfield." My shoulder teasingly bumps his, and he mock growls, pinning me to the velvet carriage bench with lust-filled eyes.

"I'm no boy, princess. I'd wager to say I'm no prince, either. Fictional or otherwise."

Swallowing thickly at the low rumble of his voice, my thighs rub together under our blanket, arousal blooming at the innuendo. As if his desires are too rough for a fair prince? As if they're too crude for a royal to speak? I desperately wish to learn the answer.

"Maybe I don't want a prince."

"Hmm... perhaps I should check?"

Check?

But his meaning becomes clear when he leans closer, his mouth hovering over mine.

"I'm going to kiss you now, Maddie," he whispers. "Because I'm just a man. A man who's fantasized about fucking you and your gorgeous curves until we pass out from exhaustion. To know the sugary taste of your cunt on my tongue, its wet grip on my cock. Does that sound like princely behavior to you?"

He swallows my answer with the press of his lips, and I forget that we're riding around Central Park where anyone could see us. Forget about the driver who could look back at any moment.

We exist in a snow globe. A magical place of winter snow, holiday lights, and passionate kisses.

Calder's palm cups my cheek and angles my head to the side for better access. He coaxes, seduces with nibbles of his teeth and swipes of his tongue until my lips part to allow him entry. It's then his demeanor changes from princely reserve to invading conqueror, taking long drags of my mouth like I'm the very oxygen he needs to breathe.

His large body turns to urge me deeper against the carriage seat, our blanket falling to the floor, permitting the brisk bite of December to sweep forward along my fiery skin.

My breasts ache against the flimsy fabric of my lingerie, needing Calder's rough handling, but he's too focused on holding me still for his plundering mouth, his fingertips digging into my hip, a bruising grip of ownership.

A honking horn and the whinnying carriage horse burst the bubble we're in seconds—*minutes, hours?* —later.

"Calder... Wait... We have to stop."

"Why?" He grumbles, pinching a love handle in reprisal. The brief shot of discomfort rockets straight to my pussy as if pain or pleasure don't matter when it comes to Calder. As long as it's his hands causing the sensation. *His* touch on my body.

"Because we're not alone."

"So? I don't give a fuck. I want you. Now."

"Language..." I reprimand though it doesn't really bother me. He could say whatever he wanted, and I'd still adore him.

"My PR team isn't here to police me, princess. That means I'm free to curse as much as I want. To fuck whoever I want. Wherever I want." He finishes the promise with another hard kiss to my lips, and I'm tempted to succumb to his possession.

It's not like the citizens of New York City will recognize me or remember that couple making out in a horse carriage. It probably happens more often than you'd think.

"Still... What if we go somewhere more private?" I broach the subject Lola and I discussed on our shopping expedition.

"Tell me you don't want to lose your virginity to Prince Charming. To your dream guy." Lola had dared, and she was right.

If ever there was a man I desired, it was Calder Mayfield. Damn the consequences. He may break my heart. I may be breaking my own heart knowing I fly home tomorrow afternoon, but it's a risk I must take. I don't think I can live the rest of my life with the regret of wondering *What if...*?

Calder retreats far enough away to meet my determined gaze. "Are you asking what I think you are? Do you want to come home with me? Or at least my home for the night?"

I nod, licking away a wayward snowflake.

"You need to say it, Maddie. I need to hear the words out loud," he demands, and if a shred of doubt remained in my heart, it would've expired in a puff of smoke from the lusty fire burning in his eyes.

"Take me to your bed, Calder. Make me yours."

And with a quick bark at the carriage driver, we head towards the Plaza Hotel—our fate sealed.

CHAPTER SIX

CALDER

The glittering lights of New York City shine through the windows of my hotel suite. I left the drapes open to the view despite the cool air seeping into the room, and I'm damn glad I did because Maddie looks like a Christmas princess, perfectly framed by the city. She exclaimed over the sparkling sight the moment we stepped into the room, immediately hurrying to the floor to ceiling windows to take it all in.

For my part, I'm still trying to rein in my control after our kiss in the carriage. Maddie tasted of coffee and cocoa from her tiramisu dessert, a sweet combination I want more of.

Her plea to be brought here—to my bed—will live etched in my memory and heart for years to come because it marks the point her trust in me deepened. Marks the moment when I realized I couldn't let her go after this weekend.

The notion lurked in the back of my mind throughout the rest of MerryCon, the ballet, and dinner. A part of me knew she was the one for me, but the logical side of my brain argued the gut feeling. Rationalized that it was just the spirit of the season. Of being surrounded by my fellow leads of romantic holiday movies. None of this could be real.

But when I kissed her, when she asked me to make her mine, those pretty eyes of hers glowing under the colorful lights decorating the carriage, I knew the truth.

Maddie's not like the women of my past.

She doesn't seek to take advantage of my name or money.

In the little time we've spent together, we've hardly spoken about my career, instead focusing on her life in Nashville, a city we both conveniently live in. About her family and mine. Normal topics between a regular man and woman getting to know each other.

"It really is beautiful." Maddie's awe is palpable, and I agree with her assessment, though I'm partial to the beauty she adds to the towers of metal and glass behind her.

"New York City isn't what fascinates me at the moment," I say, walking close enough to cage her against the window with my arms bracketing her body. "You are."

A soft gasp of surprise puffs from her pursed lips, and I swiftly breathe it in, my mouth covering hers in an insistent demand. "I want to see what you're hiding under this gown. As pretty as it is, these sexy curves have haunted me for the past twenty-four hours. My curiosity desires satisfaction. Will you strip for me, princess? Show me what you're giving me tonight."

For life.

Maddie slowly nods and reaches for a hidden zipper at her side. It easily slides down her waist and hips, loosening the twinkling fabric. Her fingers scrunch the skirt in her palms, lifting up until she's able to pull it overhead and toss it aside, revealing a surprise gift.

"Did you get this for me?" I tap the silk shaping her breasts into plump offerings that I'm hungry to taste.

Surely, she doesn't usually travel with luggage full of sexy lingerie. Right? I dismiss the idea immediately, unwilling to picture her dressed this way for another man.

"And for me," she says, sweeping a hand over her curves. The emerald corset and garter belt match the color of her discarded dress, hugging her breasts and hips. "Though you came to mind as well. Lola convinced me to buy it since it goes with my gown."

"Thank god for Lola."

"I'll tell her you said that." She laughs, but then hesitancy overcomes her. "Can I undress you now?"

Grinning, I nod and wait for her first move. Maddie eyes me up and down before her hands go to my belt, the easiest item to remove. "You're going to have to raise your arms so I can get rid of your shirt and jacket," she says, and I willingly comply, enjoying the feel of her smaller hands pushing the linen and wool from my shoulders. Adoring the cute exclamation when she shyly traces a finger down my chest and abs.

"You have to work out a lot for your roles, hmm?"

"Tool of the trade. Casting directors want beach bodies for characters, even if there has been a push for more body diversity in the past few years. Personally, I wouldn't mind playing opposite you in a film. We could get up to all sorts of trouble on set."

Maddie's brows rise in disbelief. "I don't think I'm cut out for acting. My memory's terrible, and body diversity or not, I doubt I fit their idea of plus-size. I've seen enough movies touted as body positive only to be let down."

"You could change that," I murmur as she unbuttons my slacks.

"Trying to disrupt my life some more, are you? Have me switch careers when I'm perfectly content where I am?"

Eyes widening, I vehemently shake my head, ready to apologize for offending her when Maddie giggles, amusement shining from her features. "Kidding. It could be fun doing a one-off with you just for the experience. Though this is all fantasy anyway. Strange banter because I have no clue how to be seductive."

"I don't know. You're doing a damn good job in my opinion." She's stripped me down to my boxer briefs, her breath ghosting over my rigid cock after she kneels at my feet. The tight fabric lowers until I'm completely bare for her perusal, and Maddie releases a sexy little hum of appreciation.

"That's a relief." The words are spoken so quietly that I wonder if they're meant for her ears alone. A comment meant to buoy her confidence as she hesitantly trails a finger down one line of the vee pointing to my cock. "You're rather large, aren't you?"

Pre-cum seeps from the mushroom head at the observation, and I can't help the hint of pride in my tone when I agree. "But you can take me. I'll make sure of it."

"As wet as I am, you've been *making sure* since the ballet..." The unexpected admission of her arousal heightens my own—her reserved shell cracking to reveal the sensual woman hiding beneath.

Her palms run up my thighs before cupping my ass and urging me forward so her tongue can lick at the shiny tip of my cock. "I probably shouldn't admit this, but that scene from the Lifetime movie where you're shirtless in gray sweatpants? That shot lives rent-free in my head. Features prominently in my dreams."

"Only fair," I grunt as her hands knead my ass, her lips sucking at random intervals along my cock. "Because this moment's going to be burned into my memory." I wrap a fist around her loose hair and tug. "Now, come here, princess. It's my turn to taste."

CHAPTER SEVEN

MADDIE

I feel powerful.

Sensual.

And my new lingerie isn't the only cause.

It's Calder.

The way he watches me with hooded eyes. The way those animalistic rumbles emanate from his chest. His desire is obvious—so clear that even an inexperienced woman like me can read the signs of a man on the edge of lust.

He stalks forward until my back presses against the glass door to his balcony, and I shiver at the shock of frosted glass. Like a predator playing with its prey, Calder dips his head to blow a wave of heat over my shoulder to fog the window, and goosebumps rise on my skin at the electric contrast between hot and cold. A feverish combination.

"What if someone sees us?" I whisper, keenly aware of my nakedness on display for the city streets below. Each patch of exposed skin stinging from being sandwiched between Calder's hard body and the chilly balcony doors.

"Let them watch." He leaves love bites down my neck and collarbone before reaching the swell of my breasts, still covered by the green silk of my corset. His teeth drag the thin barrier lower until my swollen nipple pops out, desperate for attention, and Calder is only too happy to please, his lips encircling the taut bud and sucking greedily.

A whimper sticks in my throat as he suckles in time with the hand diving between my thighs, his fingers toying with my clit through the damp silk. "Naughty little princess," he growls. "Soaking this pretty silk with your juicy cunt. Will you do the same to my face, I wonder?" Stooping to the carpet, he releases my nipple to playfully bite at my covered pussy. "You smell fucking delicious. My Christmas treat for being good this year."

My hands tangle in his hair, and I arch my hips, begging to be devoured by him. I want to be his princess. His reward. To be seen as a precious prize in his eyes.

Fear of rejection is so far from my mind that it almost seems like another lifetime—another woman who felt that way. Because this man has a talent for snaring my every thought, refusing to leave room for such things as fears or doubts.

The first hot swipe of his tongue on my panty-covered pussy makes me breathless.

The second makes me cry out in sweet agony.

Calder teases me through the fabric before ripping it away and burying his face between my thighs with an animalistic snarl. His thumbs separate my slick folds, the cool rush of air hardly helping the rising tide of heat in my blood as his cheeks scratch at the delicate skin, his tongue hungrily lapping up every drop of my arousal.

"Calder... Mmm... There, don't stop..." I almost expect a cocky remark or a smug grin at my pleading, but none is forthcoming. Like a gentleman—no, a *prince*—he listens and focuses on the sensitive point of my pleasure, keeping constant friction with my clit.

Impatient and half-mad with need, I brace my leg on his shoulder and grind harder into him, moaning at the rough texture of his bearded chin, until finally the building tension breaks. My toes curl into the carpet as I shudder under the crash of my orgasm, and pure bliss radiates inside me—body and soul.

All evening has led to this.

Hell, I feel like every movie I've watched of Calder's has led to this. My crush growing each year. My dreams becoming more intimate—refusing to abate just because of the difference in our social status.

Reality is much better than fantasy, though.

"You did so well, princess," Calder murmurs against my inner thigh. Slowly he comes to a stand but not before leaving his mark along my body with more nips and kisses.

"Um... you did, too." *Stupid.* I can't believe I just said that. But he just chuckles, nuzzling my ear.

"Glad you think so. How about I try for extra credit, hmm?" He hauls me into his arms, surprising me with his strength, and carries me to the bed where I'm gently placed on the end of the mattress.

Calder bunches the corset under my breasts so the heavy globes are propped up to an indecent height. Satisfied with his adjustment, he guides me to my back, leaving my feet to dangle over the side of the bed, toes barely grazing the floor.

"Comfortable, princess?"

I nod. I'm completely at his mercy, but it doesn't frighten me.

Though this position prevents me from doing much more than accepting whatever's next—my body unable to find purchase to buck against him—it's oddly freeing.

Until his hands wrap beneath my knees and bend them to my chest, leaving me vulnerable to his gaze.

Logically, I know it's nothing to be embarrassed about. The man just had his mouth on my pussy; he's seen me squished up against the window.

But I'm keenly aware of the rolls of my belly squeezed tight against my bent legs. Self-conscious about my pussy being on open display under the city lights pervading the room.

"Maybe—" I start to suggest a different pose, one that doesn't have me rolled into a squashed ball of excess padding and cellulite, but Calder's voice overpowers mine.

"You take my breath away, Maddie. All sweet curves meant to pillow me in their supple warmth. A gorgeous woman I doubt I'll ever get enough of."

Well, when he says it like that...

Puts my insecurities to shame. Because clearly, we have two different points of view, and frankly, I prefer his.

"*Threal...*" Ugh, annoying tangled tongue. "I was stuck between double-checking with a *really?* or just thanking you, and that mess came out instead."

A tender smile softens Calder's sharp features, and he leans forward to brush a smooth kiss over my lips.

"I adore how tongue-tied you can be, despite it usually being caused by nerves. But you don't need to worry, princess. Everything about you entices me. From this pink nail polish..." He tweaks my pinky toe. "To the way your eyes waver between golden and copper depending on your mood, the amber color never settling."

Oh my god, he's going to make me cry.

He's so sincere. His compliments so endearing. A man's never commented on something they liked about me outside my responsible nature or maybe a good catch on a small mistake, so Calder's words are like the first fall of rain on parched soil.

I'm thirsty for more.

The steel length of his cock slides between my separated folds to nestle into my slick opening. "And don't get me started on this pretty little pussy... You're too damn sweet to be real, and I know you're gonna milk me so good, aren't you?"

God, yes.

I want to please him in all things. From prompting one of his bellowing laughs to satisfying his hunger in bed.

Thank goodness my thick vibrator at home has done the work of ensuring there will be nothing but pleasure from Calder's possession.

Don't forget to thank birth control, too.

"Take me, Calder. I need you now. Hard and deep, nothing between us."

Just a man and a woman coming together—even if it's only for one night of lust and love.

CHAPTER EIGHT

CALDER

You don't have to tell me twice.

With a thrust of my hips, I plunge forward with a growl of pleasure. Because whatever my girl needs, she gets.

I catch a swaying nipple with my teeth and suckle the cherry tip, imagining its pretty pink deepening to red. I wasn't lying when I told Maddie how much her body fascinates me, but it's more than just a physical response I have to her charms.

She's also funny and kind and heartbreakingly sensitive—attuned to others' feelings in a way I've never experienced. I recognized that quality in her after our first messages when she checked in on me amidst the crowd of fans.

Maddie gasps as my cock drags across a particularly responsive spot in her pussy, and I place more of my weight on her to gain enough leverage to angle harder strokes against it. My pelvis rasps over her clit in a rough pattern until I feel the tightening of her muscles, her breath suspended in her lungs.

"That's it. Come for me, princess. Drench my dick with this juicy cunt. I want to hear the sloppy sounds of your sex taking every inch of me as you scream my name." I'm usually not so crude in bed, but something about Maddie brings out the base caveman who only wants to voice the filthiest demands.

Fortunately, she doesn't seem to mind. In fact, I think she kind of loves it because her body immediately obeys, clenching one final time before her orgasm erupts, releasing all of her pent-up tension.

And like an obedient little princess, my name echoes in the room as she cries out, "Calder!"

I'll never tire of hearing that exact tone of wonder and satisfaction ringing through her voice. She's the only woman I want to please. The only one I want in my bed.

A couple of jerky thrusts later, I fill her with thick ropes of cum, claiming her as my own with each drop of my seed. We lay breathless and replete until a slight groan vibrates from Maddie, and I ease out of her, gently straightening her legs from their bent position.

Not wanting to be away from her for too long, I hurry to the bathroom for a washcloth to clean us up and make quick work of the task before joining her in bed, cuddling close.

Maddie covers a yawn with her hand and sleepily blinks up at me. Clearly, I've worn her out tonight. With the ballet. Dinner. Carriage ride. And explosive sex.

Fatigue's threatening to pull me under as well, but there's something I need to say first.

"I don't want this to be our only night together, Maddie. I know you leave tomorrow at noon, but it won't be the end between us. I won't let it." I brand the promise into her skin, sealing it with a kiss before cupping Maddie's chin and drawing her gaze up to mine. "Tell me you believe me."

Because I yearn for her confirmation. This can't end with MerryCon.

A cloud of concern sweeps aways some of her drowsiness as she considers my words. "I trust that *you* believe it. Because you're sweet and generous and you don't want to hurt me."

Maddie covers my mouth when I prepare a rebuttal. "But... I went into this understanding that it'll probably only be a one-time thing. You're a movie star, after all. And I'm... well, I'm not."

"We live in the same city. We can make it work. If anything, that fact alone should convince you we're meant to be."

"As much as I'd love to think we're living a fairytale or at least a Hallmark romance, I want to be realistic. And I don't want this weekend to be spoiled by commitments made with good intentions but are ultimately just that: *intentions* not actions."

She wants action? I have no problem with showing her how deep I'm in this.

"I'll prove that you're more than just a fling, princess. Get ready to be bombarded by messages, calls, gifts, you name it. I won't let you forget me, forget about us."

"I never said I'd forget anything," she murmurs, a hand moving to massage my bicep. I think I see hope bloom in her eyes, but she nuzzles into my chest, hiding the possibility.

It was there. You saw it.

"Good, because you're mine, Maddie. You gave yourself to me, and I don't take that lightly." And I won't let her retract the gift.

Something soft that sounds like "I hope so" whispers in the air, and I tuck Maddie closer, imprinting my body on hers as we fall asleep.

Don't worry, princess. You can trust in me.

IT'S BEEN THREE MONTHS since I last saw my girl.

Three months of filming a summer movie in Italy and dreaming about Maddie.

But it's finally a wrap, and I'm home in Nashville for the first time since before MerryCon. Which means it's time for a grand gesture because I'm in love.

Every message.

Every call.

Every example of Maddie's doubt dissolving as she became more and more animated in our conversations.

It's all resulted in my heart not belonging to me anymore but her.

Knocking on Maddie's apartment door, I wipe a sweaty palm down my slacks and shift my hold on the tulips I bought—her favorite flower. She appears a minute later, surprise written on her adorable features, and my body locks up at the sight.

She's so damn beautiful.

And mine.

I pull her to me without a word, kissing her with all the constrained desire I've held back for months, making do with fucking hand jobs in the shower whenever I couldn't get Maddie out of my head.

Which was all the damn time.

"Calder, what are you doing here? I thought you said your flight didn't land until tomorrow."

"I switched flights. I couldn't be away from you any longer." Tossing the bouquet aside in favor of wrapping both arms around my woman, I confess, "I love you, Maddie. You're my dream come to life, the princess I imagined in every royal movie I've ever done."

An elated smile brightens her face as she runs a hand through my longer hair. "I love you, too. At first, I was scared because you know how reluctant I was to expect more after MerryCon. But you didn't give me enough time to doubt. Not with all our talks and your gifts, which you really didn't have to buy me, by the way."

"I *told* you I wouldn't let you forget me... Next time? Trust me, princess." I swat her round ass in playful reprimand, reveling in the feel of all her curves crushed to my hardness again.

"Oh, I trust you," She admits with a mischievous twinkle in her eyes. "You're my Prince Charming but better than any fictional man could be. Why don't you get in here, so I can give you a proper welcome home?"

We stumble back into her apartment, hastily slamming the door shut, and it's the best damn welcome I've had in a long time.

My princess, my love.

Looks like this Hallmark golden boy finally got his leading lady.

EPILOGUE ONE

MADDIE
FIVE YEARS LATER

"And that's a wrap! Good job everyone! Especially you, Mrs. Mayfield." The film director winks at me before shuffling off set with the rest of the crew.

After years of cajoling, Calder finally got me—and the network—to film a holiday movie with the two of us. I've seen countless films where the leading stars were picked from the street by a random casting director, so I finally gave in, figuring if they could do it, I could, too.

Granted, I don't plan on making it my career or anything but acting opposite my adoring husband is extremely fun and romantic.

"Yes, excellent work, Mrs. Mayfield." Calder hugs me from behind as we study the location of our final scene—a Christmas tree farm glittering under the night sky.

I played the struggling tree farm owner while Calder was the secret royal who promised to help me bring it back to life, all while I learned how to deal with dating a prince.

It's cute and silly, and I love it.

"You weren't so bad yourself, and now you can stop pestering me about our very own Hallmark movie," I tease, loving the confidence he has in me.

Calder whispers in my ear. "Hang on, I've got an idea for a sequel..."

I laugh in delight because that's my husband. Never once has he made me feel less than because of my size, anxiety, or the awkward way I combine words. His belief in me never wavers.

Because he loves me as I am—my true Prince Charming.

EPILOGUE TWO

ELI COOPER

*T*hank god another MerryCon is over.

I don't understand everyone's obsession with these damn holiday movies.

They're all the same from the predictable plot to the carbon-copy characters. It's all bullshit.

People don't act like that in real life, and Christmas isn't some happy season meant to bring couples together. But of course, if I ever voiced my annoyance with the films, I'd be out of a job.

Because somehow my career's landed me as a rom-com staple these past few years.

So, I put on a happy face and do my job like any other citizen even if the scripts make me cringe.

"They loved you, Eli." My manager says as he types away on his phone. "You've already been asked to return next year, and I'm sending your confirmation."

Great.

"Can't I take a break? Surely missing one event won't derail any role offerings." It'd be nice to spend December at home where I can avoid overly zealous holiday fans, music, decorations. Hell, the whole season really.

"No, you have to go. Especially since you'll be promoting a new holiday film around that weekend." He pulls a manuscript out of his bag on the car floor and tosses it to me.

The Little Drummer Brigade.
I read the ridiculous summary and scoff.
Fuck me.

.

THANKS FOR READING & DON'T FORGET TO RATE/ REVIEW!

Please consider leaving a rating/review on Amazon, Goodreads, Instagram, TikTok, and/or any other sites you review on.
Ratings & reviews are the #1 way to support an indie author like me.
They don't have to be long or even positive (though I hope you enjoyed this book!). All the algorithms care about are QUANTITY.
The more reviews, the more my books are shown to other potential readers!
And they serve as guides to readers on whether or not to take a chance on an indie author.
I appreciate your support!

XO, Hallie

ABOUT THE AUTHOR

Hallie prefers steamy, insta-love stories where curvy girls are claimed by filthy-talking heroes. And when she ran out of reading material, she decided to write her own stories. If you want a quick, hot read, she's your girl!

www.ingramcontent.com/pod-product-compliance
Lightning Source LLC
Chambersburg PA
CBHW030357180626
46812CB00007B/2929